For Laura

Ladybird books are widely available, but in case of difficulty may be ordered by post or telephone from:

Ladybird Books – Cash Sales Department Littlegate Road Paignton Devon TQ3 3BE
Telephone 01803 554761

A catalogue record for this book is available from the British Library

Published by Ladybird Books Ltd Loughborough Leicestershire UK
Ladybird Books Inc Auburn Maine 04210 USA

Benedict
goes to the beach

by Chris Demarest

Picture
Ladybird

It was hot in the city. Too hot for Benedict.
"I'm going to the beach," he said.

"But it's too hot to fly!" moaned his brothers and sister. "We're not coming."

"Fine. I'll go on my own," said Benedict
huffily. And off he flew.

In no time at all he spotted some big umbrellas.
"This beach is very crowded," thought Benedict.

"It's much too noisy… and there's no sand."

So off he flew.

"Ah," sighed Benedict. "A quiet spot...

…and what nice sand."

But this beach moved.

VAROOM! And Benedict tumbled off.

Then Benedict spotted some seagulls.
"They'll help me find a beach," he thought.

But the seagulls ignored him.

And anyway…

...their beach stank. *PHEW-EE!*

Poor Benedict was hotter than ever.
He was having no luck at all, until…

…he spotted a giant fish. Surely a fish would know the way to the beach. So off he flew.

But this fish would have nothing to do
with Benedict.

It swooped and spiralled. Then it swatted
Benedict with its tail. Down he tumbled…

...*KERPLONK!*
Right on to his brothers' and sister's blanket.

"You were right, Benedict," they sang. "The beach is the place to be. We've been waiting for you!"

Benedict beamed and wiggled his toes in the
sand. He was happy and cool at last.

Then they all ate... and played... and swam...

…until it was time to sail home.

Picture Ladybird

Books for reading aloud with 2–6 year olds

The *Picture Ladybird* range is full of exciting stories and rhymes that are perfect to read aloud and share. There is something for everyone – animal stories, bedtime stories, rhyming stories – and lots more!

Ten titles for you to collect

WISHING MOON AGE 3+
written & illustrated by Lesley Harker

Persephone Brown wanted to be BIG. All she ever saw were feet and knees – it really wasn't on. Then one special night her wish came true. Persephone Brown just grew and grew and *GREW*...

DON'T WORRY WILLIAM AGE 3+
by Christine Morton
illustrated by Nigel McMullen

It's a sleepy dark night. A creepy dark night. A night for naughty bears to creep downstairs and have an adventure. But, going in search of biscuits to make them brave, Horace and William hear a bang–a very loud bang–an On-The-Stairs bang! Whatever can it be?

BENEDICT GOES TO THE BEACH AGE 3+
written & illustrated by Chris Demarest

It's hot in the city – *really* hot. Poor Benedict just *has* to cool off. There is only one thing for it, head for the beach – *any* beach! Deciding is the easy part – getting there is another matter altogether...

TOOT! LEARNS TO FLY AGE 3+
by Geraldine Taylor & Jill Harker
illustrated by Georgien Overwater

It's time for Toot to learn to fly, to try and zoom across the sky. First there's take off – watch it – steady! Whoops! Bump! He's not quite ready! Follow Toot's route across the sky and see if he ever *does* learn to fly!

JOE AND THE FARM GOOSE AGE 2+
by Geraldine Taylor & Jill Harker
illustrated by Jakki Wood

A perfect way to introduce young children to farmyard life. There is lots to see and talk about – pigs and their piglets, cows and sheep, hens in the barn – and Joe's special friend – a very inquisitive goose!

THE STAR THAT FELL AGE 3+
by Karen Hayles
illustrated by Cliff Wright

When a star falls from the night sky, Fox and all the other animals want its precious warmth and brightness. When Dog finds the star he gives it to his friend Maddy. But as Maddy's dad tells her, all stars belong to the sky, and soon she must give it back.

TELEPHONE TED AGE 3+
by Joan Stimson
illustrated by Peter Stevenson

When Charlie starts playgroup poor Ted is left sitting at home like a stuffed toy. It's not much fun being a teddy on your own with no one to talk to. But then – *brring, brring* – the telephone rings, and that's when Ted's adventure begins.

JASPER'S JUNGLE JOURNEY AGE 3+
written & illustrated by Val Biro

What's behind those rugged rocks? A lion wearing purple socks! Just one of the strange sights Jasper encounters as he goes in search of his lost teddy bear. A delightful rhyming story full of jungle surprises!

SHOO FLY SHOO! AGE 4+
by Brian Moses
illustrated by Trevor Dunton

If a fly flies by and it's bothering you, just swish it and swash it and tell it to *shoo!* Trace the trail of the buzzing, zuzzing fly in this gloriously silly rhyming story.

GOING TO PLAYGROUP AGE 2+
by Geraldine Taylor & Jill Harker
illustrated by Terry McKenna

Tom's day at playgroup is full of exciting activities. He's a cook, a mechanic, a pirate and a band leader... he even flies to the moon! Ideal for children starting playgroup and full of ideas for having fun at home, too!